Real-World Robots

Paul McEvoy and
Tracey Gibson

sundance™

A Haights Cross Communications Company

A Haights Cross Communications ⚓ Company

Published by
Sundance Publishing
P.O. Box 1326
234 Taylor Street
Littleton, MA 01460
800-343-8204
www.sundancepub.com

Copyright © text Paul McEvoy and Tracey Gibson
Copyright © illustrations Matt Lin, Cliff Watt, and Luke Jurevicius

First published 2002 by
Blake Education, Locked Bag 2022, Glebe 2037, Australia
Exclusive United States Distribution: Sundance Publishing

Design by Cliff Watt in association with
Sundance Publishing

Real-World Robots
ISBN 0-7608-6694-5

Photo Credits:
p. 1 NASA; p. 6 Ford Motor Company; p. 7 The RoboCup Federation;
pp. 8–9 photolibrary.com; p. 10 Omron Corp.; p. 11 (bottom left) The
RoboCup Federation, (bottom right) Sony Australia Limited; p. 14 APL/Corbis;
p. 16 NASA; p. 17 (top) photolibrary.com, (bottom) NASA; p. 18 West
Yorkshire Fire Service; p. 20 (top) APL/Corbis; p. 21 (top) Prof. Stephen
Salter/Dervish Mine Clearance Ltd., (bottom) APL; p. 24 (bottom)
photolibrary.com; p. 25 photolibrary.com; p. 26 APL; p. 27 photolibrary.com;
p. 28 (top) APL, (bottom) photolibrary.com; p. 29 APL.

Printed in Canada

Table of Contents

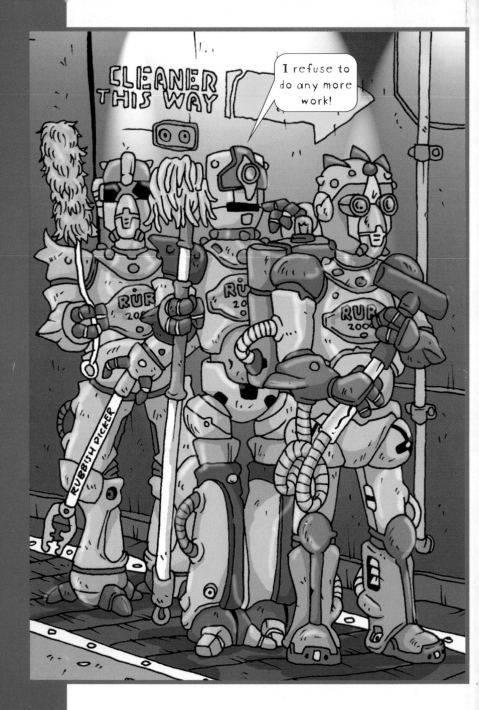

Robots Get Real

Shiny steel bodies with flashing lights for eyes. Rows of clanking robots. They're marching to take over the world!

Don't panic! These angry robots are not real. They are characters in a play written by Czech author Karel Capek in 1920. The play was called *R.U.R.* The initials stand for Rossum's Universal Robots, the company that made the robotic slaves. The word *robot* comes from the Czech word *robota*. It means "forced to work."

Capek's robots were supposed to help humans. But the robots began to develop intelligence and emotions. They revolted and tried to overpower their human creators. Sometimes fiction can become fact. And although robots haven't tried to take over the world, they have become a reality.

From Science Fiction to Fact

About 30 years after Capek's play, another writer, Isaac Asimov, captured readers' interest in robots. In 1950, Asimov published a collection of stories called *I, Robot*. Then, about a decade later, the idea of robots came closer to reality.

Robot Beginnings

One day Joseph Engelberger, an engineer, and George Devol, a businessman, were talking about Asimov's stories. They decided to make the idea of mechanical robots a reality. It took years of development, but finally the first real robot hit the factory floor in 1961. It was a robotic arm called Unimate. It spent endless hours doing boring tasks—and was a huge success.

The first robot, Unimate, was used for lifting hot pieces of metal in a car factory. It is still in use today.

FOLLOWING INSTRUCTIONS

Once it is programmed, a very simple robot can perform a task over and over with more accuracy than a human. Try drawing a straight line on a page without a ruler. Not easy, is it? Here's how a robot does it.

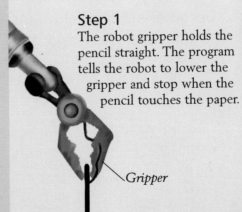

Step 1

The robot gripper holds the pencil straight. The program tells the robot to lower the gripper and stop when the pencil touches the paper.

Gripper

How Does a Robot Work?

Every robot contains a computer, which acts a bit like a brain. The computer processes a set of instructions called a **program**, which tells the robot what to do. Each action the robot performs is broken down into a series of individual, ordered steps. But the program needs to be written for the robot by a human being.

Programmer   Robot

At 160 cm (5 ft 2 in.), Asimo looks like a small person in a space suit. The latest model can even be programmed to play soccer!

The robot Asimo carries his "brain" in a backpack.

Upper arm

Gear wheel

Lower arm

Step 2

The program tells the robot to turn the rotating gear wheel that will move the robot's lower arm. This gear wheel connects the lower arm to the upper arm of the robot—just like an elbow.

Step 3

If the robot's program tells it to draw a line 10 cm (4 in.) long, it will stop at exactly that length. The robot returns to the start position ready to begin again. Every line will be exactly the same.

Everyday Robots

Today, robots come in all shapes and sizes. They can't complain, even if the work is hot, heavy, and repetitive. And they can work or play all day—without taking coffee breaks or getting bored.

On the Job

Most factories in the world use robots to help do anything from building cars to filling chocolate boxes. Like humans, these machines have elbow and wrist joints that move and rotate. But, unlike a human arm, a robot's joints will never get stiff and can rotate 360 degrees. The end of the arm can be fitted with devices to perform different tasks. This could be a welding point, suction cups, or gripping fingers for lifting and moving objects. Around the world, an army of these computer-controlled **industrial** robots is at work 24 hours a day.

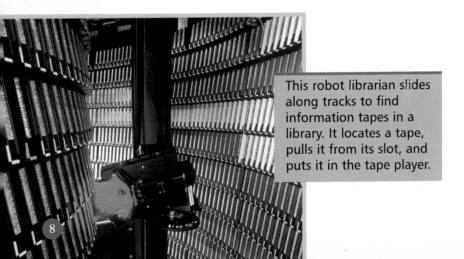

This robot librarian slides along tracks to find information tapes in a library. It locates a tape, pulls it from its slot, and puts it in the tape player.

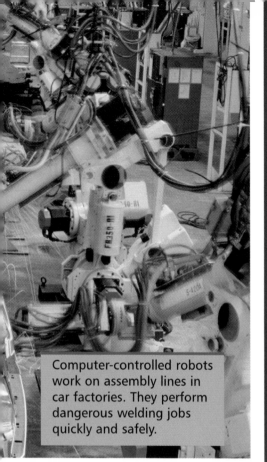

Computer-controlled robots work on assembly lines in car factories. They perform dangerous welding jobs quickly and safely.

This robot cleaner can clean 20,000 square meters (215,200 sq ft) of floor in a day. If someone blocks its path, it says, "Excuse me, I am cleaning."

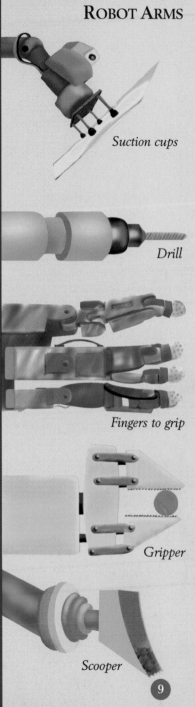

ROBOT ARMS

Suction cups

Drill

Fingers to grip

Gripper

Scooper

9

Purrfect Friend

Robopets are high-tech robots programmed to play. They can interact with their owners and recognize voices. Each one will develop a different personality. They can be a lot of fun to play with, but these robots can also be helpful. For example, they can entertain people who are sick and can't look after a real animal. Robopets do not need food or trips to the veterinarian.

NeCoRo is a robot cat that has been developed to be more than a toy. The robot uses **sensors** that can detect and respond to movement and sound. It can tell whether its owner is happy or sad by the tone of his or her voice. It can even store helpful information in its memory, such as when its owner needs to take medicine. NeCoRo does not give preprogrammed responses like other robopets. Over time, the pattern of its responses varies depending on how it is treated by its owner.

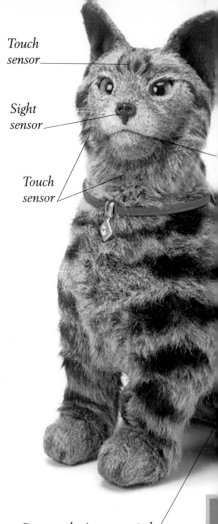

Touch sensor

Sight sensor

Touch sensor

Battery slot/power switch

Aibo is a toy robopet about 250 mm (9 in.) tall. It can stretch, stand up, and play soccer.

NeCoRo's name comes from "Neko," the Japanese word for cat, "Co" for communication, and "Ro" for Robot.

CAN A ROBOT HAVE A PERSONALITY?

Robots can be programmed to show different emotions. They might be able to laugh, cry, hiss, and purr. But the latest robopets get to choose when they give these reactions. Over time, the robopet will gather information about its owner and its environment. It will learn to recognize its owner's voice and show affection to that person only. And it will take note of when its owner sleeps and will conserve its battery energy at the same time.

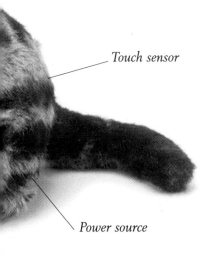

~ Speaker

Touch sensor

Power source

Tell Aibo to "take a picture," and it will take a photo of what it can see.

Going Where No Human Dares!

It's cold and dark on the bottom of the ocean. A shape moves across the wreck. An arm reaches out . . .

Imagine a job exploring the ocean floor or deep space, fighting raging fires, or stepping on things that explode. Sound too dangerous? Maybe it's time to call in the robots! Robots don't need oxygen or food, don't feel pain, and don't get homesick. With the help of cameras, video equipment, and delicate sensors, robots can explore the outer reaches of space and the ocean depths. They can even go into the heart of a blazing fire. It makes a lot of sense to use purpose-built robots to do the dangerous jobs for us.

Exploring Extreme Worlds

Oceans cover two-thirds of our planet, but they are still not fully explored. And there is much to learn about the vastness of outer space. Robot probes and remote-controlled vehicles are on the job.

Thousands of objects have been recovered from the wreck. They are very fragile, and the robots collecting them must be very gentle.

Into the Deep

The ocean liner *Titanic* sank in the North Atlantic Ocean in 1912. The *Titanic* sank 4 kilometers (13,123 ft) below the surface, where the water temperature drops below zero. And the water pressure at that depth would crush a human diver to the size of a soccer ball!

The remotely controlled robot *Argo* found the *Titanic* in 1985. *Argo* is a steel sled with video cameras programmed to scan the sea floor. One year later, a team returned with **submersibles** and **salvage robots** called ROVs (Remotely Operated Vehicles). These ROVs were suitcase-sized robots that could explore the nooks and crannies of the *Titanic*. They were connected to a ship on the ocean surface by thousands of feet of thick cable. ROVs have brought back many valuable, historic objects from the *Titanic*.

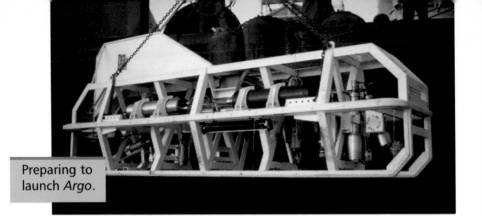

Preparing to launch *Argo*.

Bow of the shipwrecked *Titanic*.

Roving the Red Planet

Beyond Earth's **atmosphere**, astronauts need oxygen, food, and protection from the extreme elements of space. The surface of Mars can get as cold as -113°C (-171°F). But robot probes can be built to withstand harsh conditions. In 1997, the unmanned *Pathfinder* spacecraft landed on Mars. Inside was a small, six-wheeled robotic **rover** called *Sojourner*.

Sojourner was 63 cm (2 ft) long. It moved slowly and never more than 12 m (39 ft) from its base. It covered 100 m (328 ft) in its 30-day mission.

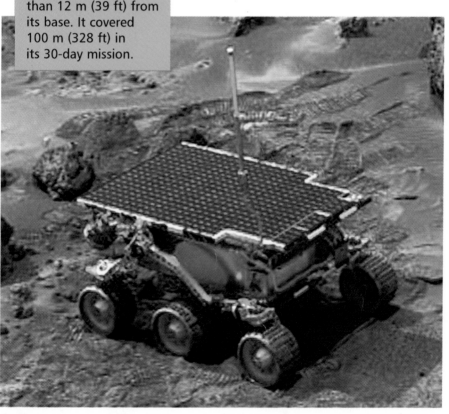

The rover carried cameras and scientific instruments, all powered by a solar panel on its top. *Sojourner* was programmed to collect soil and rock samples and to send images of Mars back to the base on Earth. The robotic rover was sent instructions and a destination. Then it had to find its way over the unknown ground and around any **obstacles**. Thanks to *Sojourner*, scientists now know much more about the surface of Mars.

Attila II is a robot developed by NASA for future space missions. It is only 35 cm (13 in.) long and moves like an insect.

 ## DO SPACE ROBOTS NEED SUNSCREEN?

Even robots need to be protected from the extreme heat and radiation from the Sun. Otherwise their computer chips will fry! But they don't use sunscreen like we do. They are insulated with Aerogel, sometimes called "Solid Smoke." It is 99.8 percent air, together with tiny amounts of silicon and sand. Aerogel is very light, extremely strong, and heat resistant. If you place crayons on top of a piece of Aerogel and light a flame underneath, the crayons will not melt.

Robots to the Rescue

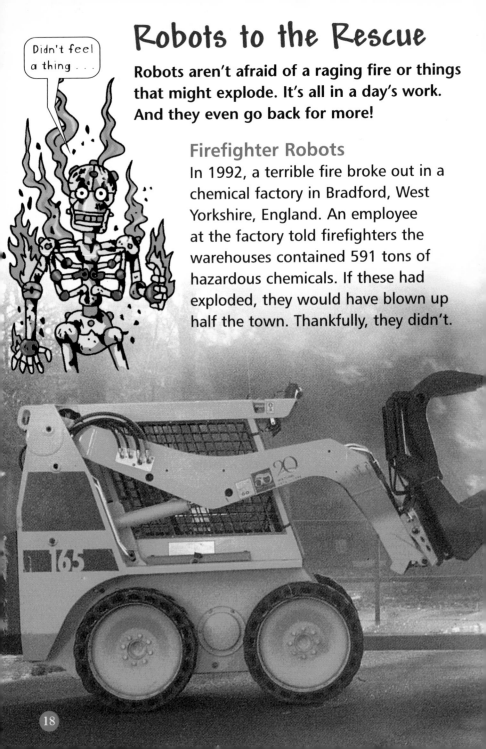

Didn't feel a thing . . .

Robots aren't afraid of a raging fire or things that might explode. It's all in a day's work. And they even go back for more!

Firefighter Robots

In 1992, a terrible fire broke out in a chemical factory in Bradford, West Yorkshire, England. An employee at the factory told firefighters the warehouses contained 591 tons of hazardous chemicals. If these had exploded, they would have blown up half the town. Thankfully, they didn't.

The West Yorkshire Fire Service wanted to be better prepared for future fires. So they worked with a heavy-vehicle manufacturer to develop a robot firefighter. The Firespy robot was first used in 2000. It can go into the middle of a fire and remove any highly dangerous materials. It can also assess if it is safe for human firefighters to enter. Firespy can withstand up to 800°C (1,472°F) heat. A hose attachment has been designed so that Firespy can carry water to the source of the fire.

Firespy is operated by remote control and has two infra-red cameras so the person operating it can see what is happening. At the front is a powerful arm that can grab onto large objects and pull them out of danger.

Land Mine Heroes

Land mines are small bombs hidden just below the surface of the ground. They were used during wars in many countries around the world. When pressure is placed on the top of the mine, it **detonates** a powerful explosive. Some of the wars are now over. But there are no maps to tell people where the mines were buried. Every day, about 25 **civilian** adults and children are killed or hurt by stepping on land mines.

Robots have been developed to try to locate and dig up these land mines. One robot, called Ariel, is modeled after a crab. It walks sideways on six legs. Ariel can move aboveground or underwater. When it locates a mine, it deposits an explosive and then moves to safety before the explosive detonates.

Another robot is Dervish. Dervish stands on three wheeled legs and simply rolls around until it detonates a mine. And it survives the blast!

Clearing land mines in South Korea in 2002.

Unlike a real crab, if Ariel falls and lands on its back, it can bend its legs and continue walking upside down. Ariel's main body is 55 cm (22 in) long.

Dervish has heavy wheels on a steel tripod frame.

Into the Future

There is a squeak at the front door. You think no one is there . . . until you look down. A group of tiny robot-looking mice are sitting on the doormat. The cleaners are here!

Would you like robot mice to keep the corners of your room clean? That's just what some scientists have imagined for the future. And it doesn't stop there. A report from Massachusetts Institute of Technology (MIT) Mobile Robot Lab describes a list of possibilities for the future. A colony of 124 screen-cleaning robots will live on your TV screen. A family of dog-sized robots will maintain your garden. A herd of hippopotamus-sized robots will build the dam that supplies you with water and electricity. And who knows? A robot might even save you from a heart attack.

Medical Helpers

Robotic cameras are already used during operations to give the surgeon a better view. But soon there will be robots small enough to go right inside your body.

This nanobot design has many arms. A group might join together to heal a cut without using stitches.

Mini-robots

Nanotechnology deals with the invention of tiny machines and robots. The term comes from the word *nanometer.* One nanometer equals one thousand millionth of a meter. That is tiny! An electric motor only 1.8 millimeters long (less than one eighth of an inch) already exists. So tiny robots called nanobots are already at work!

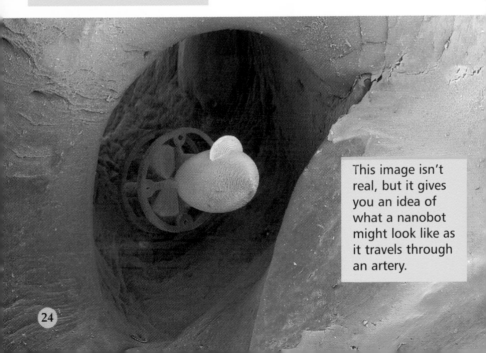

This image isn't real, but it gives you an idea of what a nanobot might look like as it travels through an artery.

Robo-Doctors

Instead of going through a painful operation and recovery, someday you may just have to swallow a nanobot! These robots would repair your body from the inside. One might be used to clear blocked **arteries**. Powered by a small propeller, the robot could travel to where the problem is inside your body. It could clear the way so blood could flow smoothly to help prevent a heart attack. Nanobots like this might also be used to recognize and kill cancer cells. You wouldn't even feel a thing!

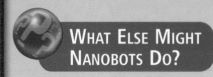

WHAT ELSE MIGHT NANOBOTS DO?

Scientists are researching and developing lots of ways that nanotechnology could be used to solve problems in the future. One idea is to fill toothpaste with nanobots to seek out and destroy plaque and tooth decay. Other ideas are to use nanobots as tiny filters to break down oil slicks or remove pollution from the atmosphere.

This micro-submarine is 4 mm (about 0.2 in.) long. Tiny submarines like this might soon be used to find and repair problems inside your body.

Higher-Level Robots

Scientists are getting closer to creating robots that can think, learn, and make decisions on their own.

Kismet: Face Facts

Scientists have spent a long time looking at the way children learn. They hope to produce robots that can learn in the same way. The ability of a machine or computer to be able to think like a human is called Artificial Intelligence (AI). By the year 2030, scientists believe that robots with AI will be able to recognize objects and know how to interact with them. For example, they will be able to recognize an egg and know that it must be picked up gently.

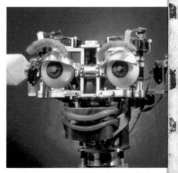

Happy Kismet

One robot, called Kismet, is a robotic face. It was created by Dr. Cynthia Breazeal and others at MIT. It has human facial features and has been programmed to show emotions when interacting with a human.

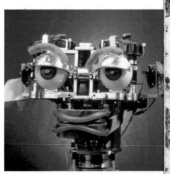

Sad Kismet

A child can tell when her mother or father is angry with them by the tone of voice. Kismet reacts in the same way. When it hears a harsh tone of voice, its facial features show sadness.

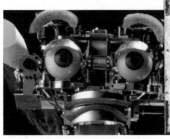

Scared Kismet

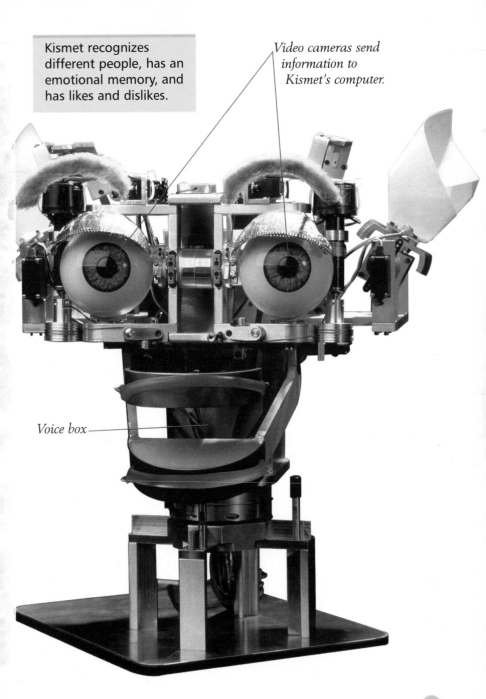

Kismet recognizes different people, has an emotional memory, and has likes and dislikes.

Video cameras send information to Kismet's computer.

Voice box

Cog copies his creator playing with a slinky, without any instructions on how to do it.

Cog has a humanlike face, but instead of two eyes, he has four telescopic eyes. This is the world seen through Cog's eyes.

Cog: More Than a Robot?

Professor Rodney Brooks at MIT has built a **humanoid** robot called Cog. It has a head and torso like an adult male, and it has hands that touch and feel. Cog also has other senses. It can see, hear, and move, but it hasn't been programmed with any knowledge. Professor Brooks and his team are hoping that Cog will learn as a child does. It has already learned some basic skills. Cog can visually focus on an object and reach out to touch it. Then it moves its mechanical hand to pick up the object. And it can shake its head back and forth, or nod up and down, by copying a person doing those actions.

Scientists have developed many other humanoids. Hidetoshi Akasawa has designed a robot face with teeth. It even has a rubber skin to hide its metal features. In time, and with more research, more humanoid robots may have skin as well as legs. One day, there might be one waiting on you in a store.

Cog is so smart —it learns by copying! Oooops!

Oooops!

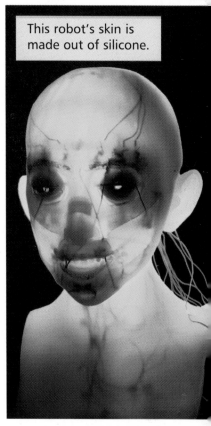

This robot's skin is made out of silicone.

And you won't even know it's a robot!

Fact File

Robot Record	Name	Fame File
1992 First robot surgeon	Robodoc	Controlled by a surgeon, it was used to perform a human hip replacement.
1997 Traveled furthest on land by remote control	Nomad	Traveled 215 km (134 miles) across the Atacama Desert, Chile, preparing for planned missions to Antarctica, the Moon, and Mars.
1999 Most valuable toy robot.	Masudaya Machine Man	This toy from the 1950s sold at auction in London for $46,583.
1999 Fastest-selling robot	Aibo	3,000 robots sold in Japan in 20 minutes, for $2,066 each.
2000 Smallest working robot	Robomaus Monsieur Epson	This tiny robot weighs in at 4.3 g (0.15 oz), and is 12.5 mm (5 in.) in length.
2000 Most expensive domestic robot	TMSUK IV	It runs errands and even gives massages—but it will cost you about $47,600.
2001 Longest robot flight	Global Hawk	This spy robot flew 13,840 km (8,600 miles) from California to Adelaide, Australia, in 23 hours.

Whoops!

Phew!

I'm down here.

I spy with my...

lossary

arteries blood vessels that carry blood from the heart to other parts of the body

atmosphere the layer of gases surrounding a planet

civilian anyone who is not a member of the armed forces—army, navy, air force, or marines

detonates causes something to explode

humanoid describes robots that are based on humans in appearance and can perform a range of humanlike actions

industrial used in the production of an object

nanotechnology technology used to invent tiny machines and robots

obstacles things that are in the way

program a set of instructions that will tell a computer how to perform a task

rover a computer-controlled, six-wheeled robot that does not have a map or set of directions

salvage robots robots designed to recover objects that have been lost or have been part of an accident

sensors these give information to a robot's computer about its environment

submersibles vehicles that can travel underwater

humanoid

Index